Little Wars

H. G. Wells

Pharos Books

ISBN: 978-93-58048-18-6
eISBN: 978-93-58048-19-3

Publisher: Pharos Books (P) Ltd.
Plot No.-63, 1st Floor, Main Mother Dairy Road
Pandav Nagar, East Delhi-110092
Phone: 011-40395855, +4049916623
WhatsApp: +91 8368220032
E-mail: sales@pharosbooks.in
Website: www.pharosbooks.in
First Edition: 2024

Printed By: Sushma Book Binding House, Okhla Industrial Area, Phase II, New Delhi-110020

Little Wars
H. G. Wells

CONTENTS

I

OF THE LEGENDARY PAST

"Little WARS" is the game of kings—for players in an inferior social position. It can be played by boys of every age from twelve to one hundred and fifty—and even later if the limbs remain sufficiently supple—by girls of the better sort, and by a few rare and gifted women. This is to be a full History of Little Wars from its recorded and authenticated beginning until the present time, an account of how to make little warfare, and hints of the most priceless sort for the recumbent strategist....

But first let it be noted in passing that there were prehistoric "Little Wars." This is no new thing, no crude novelty; but a thing tested by time, ancient and ripe in its essentials for all its perennial freshness—like spring. There was a Someone who fought Little Wars in the days of Queen Anne; a garden Napoleon. His game was inaccurately observed and insufficiently recorded by Laurence Sterne. It is clear that Uncle Toby and Corporal Trim were playing Little Wars on a scale and with an elaboration exceeding even the richness and beauty of the contemporary game. But the curtain is drawn back only to tantalise us. It is scarcely conceivable that anywhere now on earth the Shandean Rules remain on record. Perhaps they were never committed to paper....

And in all ages a certain barbaric warfare has been waged with soldiers of tin and lead and wood, with the weapons of the wild, with the catapult, the elastic circular garter, the peashooter, the rubber ball, and such-like appliances—a mere setting up and knocking down of men. Tin murder. The advance of civilisation has swept such rude contests altogether from the playroom. We know them no more....

• • •

II

THE BEGINNINGS OF MODERN LITTLE WARFARE

The beginning of the game of Little War, as we know it, became possible with the invention of the spring breechloader gun. This priceless gift to boyhood appeared somewhen towards the end of the last century, a gun capable of hitting a toy soldier nine times out of ten at a distance of nine yards. It has completely superseded all the spiral-spring and other makes of gun hitherto used in playroom warfare. These spring breechloaders are made in various sizes and patterns, but the one used in our game is that known in England as the four-point-seven gun. It fires a wooden cylinder about an inch long, and has a screw adjustment for elevation and depression. It is an altogether elegant weapon.

It was with one of these guns that the beginning of our war game was made. It was at Sandgate—in England.

SHOWING A COUNTRY PREPARED FOR THE WAR GAME.

The houses are made of wall-paper with painted doors and windows, the roofs are cut out of packing paper, and the houses are filled with wooden toy bricks to make them solid. The castle and the church are made from brown cardboard. There is a river chalked across the centre of the battlefield, which widens to flow past the great rocks in the centre. A ford is marked near the church.

SHOWING COUNTRIES PREPARED FOR THE WAR GAME.

The present writer had been lunching with a friend—let me veil his identity under the initials J. K. J.—in a room littered with the irrepressible debris of a small boy's pleasures. On a table near our own stood four or five soldiers and one of these guns. Mr J. K. J., his more urgent needs satisfied and the coffee imminent, drew a chair to this little table, sat down, examined the gun discreetly, loaded it warily, aimed, and hit his man. Thereupon he boasted of the deed, and issued challenges that were accepted with avidity....

He fired that day a shot that still echoes round the world. An affair—let us parallel the Cannonade of Valmy and call it the Cannonade of Sandgate—occurred, a shooting between opposed ranks of soldiers, a shooting not very different in spirit—but how different in results!—from the prehistoric warfare of catapult and garter. "But suppose," said his antagonists; "suppose somehow one could move the men!" and therewith opened a new world of belligerence.

The matter went no further with Mr J. K. J. The seed lay for a time gathering strength, and then began to germinate with another friend, Mr W. To Mr W. was broached the idea: "I believe that if one set up a few obstacles on the floor, volumes of the British Encyclopedia and so forth, to make a Country, and moved these soldiers and guns about, one could have rather a good game, a kind of kriegspiel."...

Primitive attempts to realise the dream were interrupted by a great rustle and chattering of lady visitors. They regarded the objects upon the floor with the empty disdain of their sex for all imaginative things.

But the writer had in those days a very dear friend, a man too ill for long excursions or vigorous sports (he has been dead now these six years), of a very sweet companionable disposition, a hearty jester and full of the spirit of play. To him the idea was broached more fruitfully. We got two forces of toy soldiers, set out a lumpish Encyclopaedic land upon the carpet, and began to play. We arranged to move in alternate moves: first one moved all his force and then the other; an infantry-man could move one foot at each move, a cavalry-man two, a gun two, and it might fire six shots; and if a man was moved up to touch another man, then we tossed up and decided which man was dead. So we made a game, which was not a good game, but which was very amusing once or twice. The men were packed under the lee of fat volumes, while the guns, animated by a spirit of their own, banged away at any exposed head, or prowled about in search of a shot. Occasionally men came into contact, with remarkable results. Rash is the man who trusts his life to the spin of a coin. One impossible paladin slew in succession nine men and turned defeat to victory, to the extreme exasperation of the strategist who had led those victims to their doom. This inordinate factor of chance eliminated play; the individual freedom of guns turned battles into scandals of crouching concealment; there was too much cover afforded by the books and vast intervals of waiting while the players took aim. And yet there was something about it.... It was a game crying aloud for improvement.

Improvement came almost simultaneously in several directions. First there was the development of the Country. The soldiers did not stand well on an ordinary carpet, the Encyclopedia made clumsy cliff-like "cover", and more particularly the room in which the game had its beginnings was subject to the invasion of callers, alien souls, trampling skirt-swishers, chatterers, creatures unfavourably impressed by the spectacle of two middle-aged men playing with "toy soldiers" on the floor, and very heated and excited about it. Overhead was the day nursery, with a wide extent of smooth cork carpet (the natural terrain of toy soldiers), a large box of bricks—such as I have described in Floor Games—and certain large inch-thick boards.

It was an easy task for the head of the household to evict his offspring, annex these advantages, and set about planning a more realistic country. (I forget what became of the children.) The thick boards were piled up one upon another to form hills; holes were bored in them, into which twigs of various shrubs were stuck to represent trees; houses and sheds (solid and compact piles of from three to six or seven inches high, and broad in proportion) and walls were made with the bricks; ponds and swamps and rivers, with fords and so forth indicated, were chalked out on the floor, garden stones were brought in to represent great rocks, and the "Country" at least of our perfected war game was in existence. We discovered it was easy to cut out and bend and gum together paper and cardboard walls, into which our toy bricks could be packed, and on which we could paint doors and windows, creepers and rain-water pipes, and so forth, to represent houses, castles, and churches in a more realistic manner, and, growing skilful, we made various bridges and so forth of card. Every boy who has ever put together model villages knows how to do these things, and the attentive reader will find them edifyingly represented in our photographic illustrations.

There has been little development since that time in the Country. Our illustrations show the methods of arrangement, and the reader will see how easily and readily the utmost variety of battlefields can be made. (It is merely to be remarked that a too crowded Country makes the guns ineffective and leads to a mere tree to tree and house to house scramble, and that large open spaces along the middle, or rivers without frequent fords and bridges, lead to ineffective cannonades, because of the danger of any advance. On the whole, too much cover is better than too little.) We decided that one player should plan and lay out the Country, and the other player choose from which side he would come. And to-day we play over such landscapes in a cork-carpeted schoolroom, from which the proper occupants are no longer evicted but remain to take an increasingly responsible and less and less audible and distressing share in the operations.

SHOWING THE WAR GAME IN THE OPEN AIR.

The soldiers stand quite well on carefully mown grass. The paper houses are loaded with wood or toy bricks as in the indoor game. Twig trees are quite easily stuck into the ground, but none are shown in these pictures. As space is less restricted, one can double the length of the moves and play with a more open country.

THE WAR GAME IN THE OPEN AIR.

We found it necessary to make certain general rules. Houses and sheds must be made of solid lumps of bricks, and not hollow so that soldiers can be put inside them, because otherwise muddled situations arise. And it was clearly necessary to provide for the replacement of disturbed objects by chalking out the outlines of boards and houses upon the floor or boards upon which they stood.

And while we thus perfected the Country, we were also eliminating all sorts of tediums, disputable possibilities, and deadlocks from the game. We decided that every man should be as brave and skilful as every other man, and that when two men of opposite sides came into contact they would inevitably kill each other. This restored strategy to its predominance over chance.

We then began to humanise that wild and fearful fowl, the gun. We decided that a gun could not be fired if there were not six—afterwards we reduced the number to four—men within six inches of it. And we ruled that a gun could not both fire and move in the same general move: it could either be fired or moved (or left alone). If there were less than six men within six inches of a gun, then we tried letting it fire as many shots as there were men, and we permitted a single man to move a gun, and move with it as far as he could go by the rules—a foot, that is, if he was an infantry-man, and two feet if he was a cavalry-man. We abolished altogether that magical freedom of an unassisted gun to move two feet. And on such rules as these we fought a number of battles. They were interesting, but not entirely satisfactory. We took no prisoners—a feature at once barbaric and unconvincing. The battles lingered on a long time, because we shot with extreme care and deliberation, and they were hard to bring to a decisive finish. The guns were altogether too predominant. They prevented attacks getting home, and they made it possible for a timid player to put all his soldiers out of sight behind hills and houses, and bang away if his opponent showed as much as the tip of a bayonet. Monsieur Bloch seemed vindicated, and Little War had become impossible. And there was something a little absurd, too, in the spectacle of a solitary drummer-boy, for example, marching off with a gun.

But as there was nevertheless much that seemed to us extremely pretty and picturesque about the game, we set to work—and here a certain Mr M. with his brother, Captain M., hot from the Great War in South Africa, came in most helpfully—to quicken it. Manifestly the guns had to be reduced to manageable terms. We cut down the number of shots per move to four, and we required that four men should be within six inches of a gun for it to be in action at all. Without four men it could neither fire nor move—it was out of action; and if it moved, the four men had to go with it. Moreover, to put an end to that little resistant body of men behind a house, we required that after a gun had been fired it should remain, without alteration of the elevation, pointing in the direction of its last shot, and have two men placed one on either side of the end of its trail. This secured a certain exposure on the part of concealed and sheltered gunners. It was no longer possible to go on shooting out of a perfect security for ever. All this favoured the attack and led to a livelier game.

Our next step was to abolish the tedium due to the elaborate aiming of the guns, by fixing a time limit for every move. We made this an outside limit at first, ten minutes, but afterwards we discovered that it made the game much more warlike to cut the time down to a length that would barely permit a slow-moving player to fire all his guns and move all his men. This led to small bodies of men lagging and "getting left," to careless exposures, to rapid, less accurate shooting, and just that eventfulness one would expect in the hurry and passion of real fighting. It also made the game brisker. We have since also made a limit, sometimes of four minutes, sometimes of five minutes, to the interval for adjustment and deliberation after one move is finished and before the next move begins. This further removes the game from the chess category, and approximates it to the likeness of active service. Most of a general's decisions, once a fight has begun, must be made in such brief intervals of time. (But we leave unlimited time at the outset for the planning.)

As to our time-keeping, we catch a visitor with a stop-watch if we can, and if we cannot, we use a fair-sized clock with a second-hand: the player not moving says "Go," and warns at the last two minutes, last minute, and last thirty seconds. But I think it would not be difficult to procure a cheap clock—because, of course, no one wants a very accurate agreement with Greenwich as to the length of a second—that would have minutes instead of hours and seconds instead of minutes, and that would ping at the end of every minute and discharge an alarm note at the end of the move. That would abolish the rather boring strain of time-keeping. One could just watch the fighting.

Moreover, in our desire to bring the game to a climax, we decided that instead of a fight to a finish we would fight to some determined point, and we found very good sport in supposing that the arrival of three men of one force upon the back line of the opponent's side of the country was of such strategic importance as to determine the battle. But this form of battle we have since largely abandoned in favour of the old fight to a finish again. We found it led to one type of battle only, a massed rush at the antagonist's line, and that our arrangements of time-limits and capture and so forth had eliminated most of the concluding drag upon the game.

Our game was now very much in its present form. We considered at various times the possibility of introducing some complication due to the bringing up of ammunition or supplies generally, and we decided that it would add little to the interest or reality of the game. Our battles are little brisk fights in which one may suppose that all the ammunition and food needed are carried by the men themselves.

But our latest development has been in the direction of killing hand to hand or taking prisoners. We found it necessary to distinguish between an isolated force and a force that was merely a projecting part of a larger force. We made a definition of isolation. After a considerable amount of trials we decided that a man or a detachment shall be considered to be isolated when there is less than half its number of its own side within a move of it. Now, in actual civilised warfare small detached bodies do not sell their lives dearly; a considerably larger force is able to make them prisoners without difficulty. Accordingly we decided that if a blue force, for example, has one or more men isolated, and a red force of at least double the strength of this isolated detachment moves up to contact with it, the blue men will be considered to be prisoners.

That seemed fair; but so desperate is the courage and devotion of lead soldiers, that it came to this, that any small force that got or seemed likely to get isolated and caught by a superior force instead of waiting to be taken prisoners, dashed at its possible captors and slew them man for man. It was manifestly unreasonable to permit this. And in considering how best to prevent such inhuman heroisms, we were reminded of another frequent incident in our battles that also erred towards the incredible and vitiated our strategy. That was the charging of one or two isolated horse-men at a gun in order to disable it. Let me illustrate this by an incident. A force consisting of ten infantry and five cavalry with a gun are retreating across an exposed space, and a gun with thirty men, cavalry and infantry, in support comes out upon a crest into a position to fire within two feet of the retreating cavalry. The attacking player puts eight men within six inches of his gun and pushes the rest of his men a little forward to the right or left in pursuit of his enemy. In the real thing, the retreating horsemen would go off to cover with the gun, "hell for leather," while the infantry would open out and retreat, firing. But see what happened in our imperfect form of Little War! The move of the retreating player began. Instead of retreating his whole force, he charged home with his mounted desperadoes, killed five of the eight men about the gun, and so by the rule silenced it, enabling the rest of his little body to get clean away to cover at the leisurely pace of one foot a move. This was not like any sort of warfare. In real life cavalry cannot pick out and kill its equivalent in cavalry while that equivalent is closely supported by other cavalry or infantry; a handful of troopers cannot gallop past well and abundantly manned guns in action, cut down the gunners and interrupt the fire. And yet for a time we found it a little difficult to frame simple rules to meet these two bad cases and prevent such scandalous possibilities. We did at last contrive to do so; we invented what we call the melee, and our revised rules in the event of a melee will be found set out upon a later page. They do really permit something like an actual result to hand-to-hand encounters. They abolish Horatius Cocles.

THE WAR GAME IN THE OPEN AIR.

FIG. 1.—BATTLE OF HOOK'S FARM. General view of the battlefield and the Red Army. (*See page 73.*)

We also found difficulties about the capturing of guns. At first we had merely provided that a gun was captured when it was out of action and four men of the opposite force were within six inches of it, but we found a number of cases for which this rule was too vague. A gun, for example, would be disabled and left with only three men within six inches; the enemy would then come up eight or ten strong within six inches on the other side, but not really reaching the gun. At the next move the original possessor of the gun would bring up half a dozen men within six inches. To whom did the gun belong? By the original wording of our rule, it might be supposed to belong to the attack which had never really touched the gun yet, and they could claim to turn it upon its original side. We had to meet a number of such cases. We met them by requiring the capturing force—or, to be precise, four men of it—actually to pass the axle of the gun before it could be taken.

All sorts of odd little difficulties arose too, connected with the use of the guns as a shelter from fire, and very exact rules had to be made to avoid tilting the nose and raising the breech of a gun in order to use it as cover....

We still found it difficult to introduce any imitation into our game of either retreat or the surrender of men not actually taken prisoners in a melee. Both things were possible by the rules, but nobody did them because there was no inducement to do them. Games were apt to end obstinately with the death or capture of the last man. An inducement was needed. This we contrived by playing not for the game but for points, scoring the result of each game and counting the points towards the decision of a campaign. Our campaign was to our single game what a rubber is to a game of whist. We made the end of a war 200, 300, or 400 or more points up, according to the number of games we wanted to play, and we scored a hundred for each battle won, and in addition 1 for each infantry-man, 1-1/2 for each cavalry-man, 10 for each gun, 1/2 for each man held prisoner by the enemy, and 1/2 for each prisoner held at the end of the game, subtracting what the antagonist scored by the same scale. Thus, when he felt the battle was hopelessly lost, he had a direct inducement to retreat any guns he could still save and surrender any men who were under the fire of the victors' guns and likely to be slaughtered, in order to minimise the score against him. And an interest was given to a skilful retreat, in which the loser not only saved points for himself but inflicted losses upon the pursuing enemy.

At first we played the game from the outset, with each player's force within sight of his antagonist; then we found it possible to hang a double curtain of casement cloth from a string stretched across the middle of the field, and we drew this back only after both sides had set out their men. Without these curtains we found the first player was at a heavy disadvantage, because he displayed all his dispositions before his opponent set down his men.

And at last our rules have reached stability, and we regard them now with the virtuous pride of men who have persisted in a great undertaking and arrived at precision after much tribulation. There is not a piece of constructive legislation in the world, not a solitary attempt to meet a complicated problem, that we do not now regard the more charitably for our efforts to get a right result from this apparently easy and puerile business of fighting with tin soldiers on the floor.

And so our laws all made, battles have been fought, the mere beginnings, we feel, of vast campaigns. The game has become in a dozen aspects extraordinarily like a small real battle. The plans are made, the Country hastily surveyed, and then the curtains are closed, and the antagonists make their opening dispositions. Then the curtains are drawn back and the hostile forces come within sight of each other; the little companies and squadrons and batteries appear hurrying to their positions, the infantry deploying into long open lines, the cavalry sheltering in reserve, or galloping with the guns to favourable advance positions.

In two or three moves the guns are flickering into action, a cavalry melee may be in progress, the plans of the attack are more or less apparent, here are men pouring out from the shelter of a wood to secure some point of vantage, and here are troops massing among farm buildings for a vigorous attack. The combat grows hot round some vital point. Move follows move in swift succession. One realises with a sickening sense of error that one is outnumbered and hard pressed here and uselessly cut off there, that one's guns are ill-placed, that one's wings are spread too widely, and that help can come only over some deadly zone of fire.

So the fight wears on. Guns are lost or won, hills or villages stormed or held; suddenly it grows clear that the scales are tilting beyond recovery, and the loser has nothing left but to contrive how he may get to the back line and safety with the vestiges of his command....

But let me, before I go on to tell of actual battles and campaigns, give here a summary of our essential rules.

• • •

III

THE RULES

Here, then, are the rules of the perfect battle-game as we play it in an ordinary room.

THE COUNTRY

1. The Country must be arranged by one player, who, failing any other agreement, shall be selected by the toss of a coin.
2. The other player shall then choose which side of the field he will fight from.
3. The Country must be disturbed as little as possible in each move. Nothing in the Country shall be moved or set aside deliberately to facilitate the firing of guns. A player must not lie across the Country so as to crush or disturb the Country if his opponent objects. Whatever is moved by accident shall be replaced after the end of the move.

THE MOVE

1. After the Country is made and the sides chosen, then (and not until then) the players shall toss for the first move.
2. If there is no curtain, the player winning the toss, hereafter called the First Player, shall next arrange his men along his back line, as he chooses. Any men he may place behind or in front of his back line shall count in the subsequent move as if they touched the back line at its nearest point. The Second Player shall then do the same. But if a curtain is available both first and second player may put down their men at the same time. Both players may take unlimited time for the putting down of their men; if there is a curtain it is drawn back when they are ready, and the game then begins.

FIG. 2.—BATTLE OF HOOK'S FARM. A near view of the Blue Army. (See page 74.)

FIG. 3.—BATTLE OF HOOK'S FARM. Positions of both armies after their first move. The Red Army is in the foreground. (See page 75.)

3. The subsequent moves after the putting down are timed. The length of time given for each move is determined by the size of the forces engaged. About a minute should be allowed for moving 30 men and a minute for each gun. Thus for a force of 110 men and 3 guns, moved by one player, seven minutes is an ample allowance. As the battle progresses and the men are killed off, the allowance is reduced as the players may agree. The player about to move stands at attention a yard behind his back line until the timekeeper says "Go." He then proceeds to make his move until time is up. He must instantly stop at the cry of "Time." Warning should be given by the timekeeper two minutes, one minute, and thirty seconds before time is up. There will be an interval before the next move, during which any disturbance of the Country

can be rearranged and men accidentally overturned replaced in a proper attitude. This interval must not exceed five or four minutes, as may be agreed upon.

4. Guns must not be fired before the second move of the first player—not counting the "putting down" as a move. Thus the first player puts down, then the second player, the first player moves, then the second player, and the two forces are then supposed to come into effective range of each other and the first player may open fire if he wishes to do so.

5. In making his move a player must move or fire his guns if he wants to do so, before moving his men. To this rule of "Guns First" there is to be no exception.

6. Every soldier may be moved and every gun moved or fired at each move, subject to the following rules:

MOBILITY OF THE VARIOUS ARMS

(Each player must be provided with two pieces of string, one two feet in length and the other six inches.)

I. An infantry-man may be moved a foot or any less distance at each move.

II. A cavalry-man may be moved two feet or any less distance at each move.

III. A gun is in action if there are at least four men of its own side within six inches of it. If there are not at least four men within that distance, it can neither be moved nor fired.

IV. If a gun is in action it can either be moved or fired at each move, but not both. If it is fired, it may fire as many as four shots in each move. It may be swung round on its axis (the middle point of its wheel axle) to take aim, provided the Country about it permits; it may be elevated or depressed, and the soldiers about it may, at the discretion of the firer, be made to lie down in their places to facilitate its handling. Moreover, soldiers who have got in front of the fire of their own guns may lie down while the guns fire over them. At the end of the move the gun must be left without altering its elevation and pointing in the direction of the last shot. And after firing, two men must be placed exactly at the end of the trail of the gun, one on either side in a line directly behind the wheels. So much for firing. If the gun is moved and not fired, then at least four men who are with the gun must move up with it to its new position, and be placed within six inches of it in its new position. The gun itself must be placed trail forward and the muzzle pointing back in the direction from which it came, and so it must remain until it is swung round on its axis to fire. Obviously the distance which a gun can move will be determined by the men it is with; if there are at least four cavalry-men with it, they can take the gun two feet, but if there are fewer cavalry-men than four and the rest infantry, or no cavalry and all infantry, the gun will be movable only one foot.

V. Every man must be placed fairly clear of hills, buildings, trees, guns, etc. He must not be jammed into interstices, and either player may insist upon a clear distance between any man and any gun or other object of at least one-sixteenth of an inch. Nor must men be packed in contact with men. A space of one-sixteenth of an inch should be kept between them.

VI. When men are knocked over by a shot they are dead, and as many men are dead as a shot knocks over or causes to fall or to lean so that they would fall if unsupported. But if a shot strikes a man but does not knock him over, he is dead, provided the shot has not already killed a man. But a shot cannot kill more than one man without knocking him over, and if it touches several without oversetting them, only the first touched is dead and the others are not incapacitated. A shot that rebounds from or glances off any object and touches a man, kills him; it kills him even if it simply rolls to his feet, subject to what has been said in the previous sentence.

HAND-TO-HAND FIGHTING AND CAPTURING

1. A man or a body of men which has less than half its own number of men on its own side within a move of it, is said to be isolated. But if there is at least half its number of men of its own side within a move of it, it is not isolated; it is supported.

2. Men may be moved up into virtual contact (one-eighth of an inch or closer) with men of the opposite side. They must then be left until the end of the move.

3. At the end of the move, if there are men of the side that has just moved in contact with any men of the other side, they constitute a melee. All the men in contact, and any other men within six inches of the men in contact, measuring from any point of their persons, weapons, or horses, are supposed to take part in the melee. At the end of the move the two players examine the melee and dispose of the men concerned according to the following rules:—

Either the numbers taking part in the melee on each side are equal or unequal.

(a) If they are equal, all the men on both sides are killed.

(b) If they are unequal, then the inferior force is either isolated or (measuring from the points of contact) not isolated.

(i) If it is isolated (see (1) above), then as many men become prisoners as the inferior force is less in numbers than the superior force, and the rest kill each a man and are killed. Thus nine against eleven have two taken prisoners, and each side seven men dead. Four of the eleven remain with two prisoners. One may put this in another way by saying that the two forces kill each other off, man for man, until one force is double the other, which is then taken prisoner. Seven men kill seven men, and then four are left with two.

(ii) But if the inferior force is not isolated (see (1) above), then each man of the inferior force kills a man of the superior force and is himself killed.

And the player who has just completed the move, the one who has charged, decides, when there is any choice, which men in the melee, both of his own and of his antagonist, shall die and which shall be prisoners or captors.

All these arrangements are made after the move is over, in the interval between the moves, and the time taken for the adjustment does not count as part of the usual interval for consideration. It is extra time.

The player next moving may, if he has taken prisoners, move these prisoners. Prisoners may be sent under escort to the rear or wherever the capturer directs, and one man within six inches of any number of prisoners up to seven can escort these prisoners and go with them. Prisoners are liberated by the death of any escort there may be within six inches of them, but they may not be moved by the player of their own side until the move following that in which the escort is killed. Directly prisoners are taken they are supposed to be disarmed, and if they are liberated they cannot fight until they are rearmed. In order to be rearmed they must return to the back line of their own side. An escort having conducted prisoners to the back line, and so beyond the reach of liberation, may then return into the fighting line.

Prisoners once made cannot fight until they have returned to their back line. It follows, therefore, that if after the adjudication of a melee a player moves up more men into touch with the survivors of this first melee, and so constitutes a second melee, any prisoners made in the first melee will not count as combatants in the second melee. Thus if A moves up nineteen men into a melee with thirteen of B's—B having only five in support—A makes six prisoners, kills seven men, and has seven of his own killed. If, now, B can move up fourteen men into melee with A's victorious survivors, which he may be able to do by bringing the five into contact, and getting nine others within six inches of them, no count is made of the six of B's men who are prisoners in the hands of A. They are disarmed. B, therefore, has fourteen men in the second melee and A twelve, B makes two prisoners, kills ten of A's men, and has ten of his own killed. But now the six prisoners originally made by A are left without an escort, and are therefore recaptured by B. But they must go to B's back line and return before they can fight again. So, as the outcome of these two melees, there are six of B's men going as released prisoners to his back line whence they may return into the battle, two of A's men prisoners in the hands of B, one of B's staying with them as escort, and three of B's men still actively free for action. A, at a cost of nineteen men, has disposed of seventeen of B's men for good, and of six or seven, according to whether B keeps his prisoners in his fighting line or not, temporarily.

FIG. 4.—BATTLE OF HOOK'S FARM. The affair is developing rapidly. (*See page 76.*)

FIG. 5A.—BATTLE OF HOOK'S FARM. Red Cavalry charging home over the Blue guns. (*See page 76.*)

(4) Any isolated body may hoist the white flag and surrender at any time.

(5) A gun is captured when there is no man whatever of its original side within six inches of it, and when at least four men of the antagonist side have moved up to it and have passed its wheel axis going in the direction of their attack. This latter point is important. An antagonist's gun may be out of action, and you may have a score of men coming up to it and within six inches of it, but it is not yet captured; and you may have brought up a dozen men all round the hostile gun, but if there is

still one enemy just out of their reach and within six inches of the end of the trail of the gun, that gun is not captured: it is still in dispute and out of action, and you may not fire it or move it at the next move. But once a gun is fully captured, it follows all the rules of your own guns.

VARIETIES OF THE BATTLE-GAME

You may play various types of game.

1. One is the Fight to the Finish. You move in from any points you like on the back line and try to kill, capture, or drive over his back line the whole of the enemy's force. You play the game for points; you score 100 for the victory, and 10 for every gun you hold or are in a position to take, 1-1/2 for every cavalry-man, 1 for every infantry-man still alive and uncaptured, 1/2 for every man of yours prisoner in the hands of the enemy, and 1/2 for every prisoner you have taken. If the battle is still undecided when both forces are reduced below fifteen men, the battle is drawn and the 100 points for victory are divided.

   Note—This game can be fought with any sized force, but if it is fought with less than 50 a side, the minimum must be 10 a side.

2. The Blow at the Rear game is decided when at least three men of one force reach any point in the back line of their antagonist. He is then supposed to have suffered a strategic defeat, and he must retreat his entire force over the back line in six moves, i.e. six of his moves. Anything left on the field after six moves capitulates to the victor. Points count as in the preceding game, but this lasts a shorter time and is better adapted to a cramped country with a short back line. With a long rear line the game is simply a rush at some weak point in the first player's line by the entire cavalry brigade of the second player. Instead of making the whole back line available for the Blow at the Rear, the middle or either half may be taken.

3. In the Defensive Game, a force, the defenders, two-thirds as strong as its antagonist, tries to prevent the latter arriving, while

still a quarter of its original strength, upon the defender's back line. The Country must be made by one or both of the players before it is determined which shall be defender. The players then toss for choice of sides, and the winner of the toss becomes the defender. He puts out his force over the field on his own side, anywhere up to the distance of one move off the middle line—that is to say, he must not put any man within one move of the middle line, but he may do so anywhere on his own side of that limit—and then the loser of the toss becomes first player, and sets out his men a move from his back line. The defender may open fire forthwith; he need not wait until after the second move of the first player, as the second player has to do.

COMPOSITION OF FORCES

Except in the above cases, or when otherwise agreed upon, the forces engaged shall be equal in number and similar in composition. The methods of handicapping are obvious. A slight inequality (chances of war) may be arranged between equal players by leaving out 12 men on each side and tossing with a pair of dice to see how many each player shall take of these. The best arrangement and proportion of the forces is in small bodies of about 20 to 25 infantry-men and 12 to 15 cavalry to a gun. Such a force can maneuver comfortably on a front of 4 or 5 feet. Most of our games have been played with about 80 infantry, 50 cavalry, 3 or 4 naval guns, and a field gun on either side, or with smaller proportional forces. We have played excellent games on an eighteen-foot battlefield with over two hundred men and six guns a side. A player may, of course, rearrange his forces to suit his own convenience; brigade all or most of his cavalry into a powerful striking force, or what not. But more guns proportionally lead to their being put out of action too early for want of men; a larger proportion of infantry makes the game sluggish, and more cavalry—because of the difficulty of keeping large bodies of this force under cover—leads simply to early heavy losses by gunfire and violent and disastrous charging. The composition of a force may, of course, be varied considerably. One good Fight to a Finish game we tried as follows: We made the Country, tossed for choice, and then drew curtains across the middle of the field. Each player then selected his force from the available soldiers in this way: he counted infantry as 1 each, cavalry as 1-1/2, and a gun as 10, and, taking whatever he liked in whatever position he liked, he made up a total of 150. He could, for instance, choose 100 infantry and 5 guns, or 100 cavalry and no guns, or 60 infantry, 40 cavalry, and 3 guns. In the result, a Boer-like cavalry force of 80 with 3 guns suffered defeat at the hands of 110 infantry with 4.

SIZE OF THE SOLDIERS

The soldiers used should be all of one size. The best British makers have standardised sizes, and sell infantry and cavalry in exactly proportioned dimensions; the infantry being nearly two inches tall. There is a lighter, cheaper make of perhaps an inch and a half high that is also available. Foreign-made soldiers are of variable sizes.

• • •

IV

THE BATTLE OF HOOK'S FARM

And now, having given all the exact science of our war game, having told something of the development of this warfare, let me here set out the particulars of an exemplary game. And suddenly your author changes. He changes into what perhaps he might have been—under different circumstances. His inky fingers become large, manly hands, his drooping scholastic back stiffens, his elbows go out, his etiolated complexion corrugates and darkens, his moustaches increase and grow and spread, and curl up horribly; a large, red scar, a sabre cut, grows lurid over one eye. He expands—all over he expands. He clears his throat startlingly, lugs at the still growing ends of his moustache, and says, with just a faint and fading doubt in his voice as to whether he can do it, "Yas, Sir!"

FIG. 5a.—BATTLE OF HOOK'S FARM. After the cavalry mêlée. (See page 60.)

FIG. 6A.—BATTLE OF HOOK'S FARM. The three Red Cavalry prisoners are being led to the rear. (*See page* 80.)

Now for a while you listen to General H. G. W., of the Blue Army. You hear tales of victory. The photographs of the battlefields are by a woman war-correspondent, A. C. W., a daring ornament of her sex. I vanish. I vanish, but I will return. Here, then, is the story of the battle of Hook's Farm.

"The affair of Hook's Farm was one of those brisk little things that did so much to build up my early reputation. I did remarkably well, though perhaps it is not my function to say so. The enemy was slightly stronger, both in cavalry and infantry, than myself [Footnote: A slight but pardonable error on the part of the gallant gentleman. The forces were exactly equal.]; he had the choice of position, and opened the ball. Nevertheless I routed him. I had with me a compact little force of 3 guns, 48 infantry, and 25 horse. My instructions were to clear up the country to the east of Firely Church.

"We came very speedily into touch. I discovered the enemy advancing upon Hook's Farm and Firely Church, evidently with the intention of holding those two positions and giving me a warm welcome. I have by me a photograph or so of the battlefield and also a little sketch I used upon the field. They will give the intelligent reader a far better idea of the encounter than any so-called 'fine writing' can do.

"The original advance of the enemy was through the open country behind Firely Church and Hook's Farm; I sighted him between the points marked A A and B B, and his force was divided into two columns, with very little cover or possibility of communication between them if once the intervening ground was under fire. I reckoned about 22 to his left and 50 or 60 to his right. [Footnote: Here again the gallant gentleman errs; this time he magnifies.] Evidently he meant to seize both Firely Church and Hook's Farm, get his guns into action, and pound my little force to pieces while it was still practically in the open. He could reach both these admirable positions before I could hope to get a man there. There was no effective cover whatever upon my right that would have permitted an advance up to the church, and so I decided to concentrate my whole force in a rush upon Hook's Farm, while I staved off his left with gun fire. I do not believe any strategist whatever could have bettered that scheme. My guns were at the points marked D C E, each with five horsemen, and I deployed my infantry in a line between D and E. The rest of my cavalry I ordered to advance on Hook's Farm from C. I have shown by arrows on the sketch the course I proposed for my guns. The gun E was to go straight for its assigned position, and get into action at once. C was not to risk capture or being put out of action; its exact position was to be determined by Red's rapidity in getting up to the farm, and it was to halt and get to work directly it saw any chance of effective fire.

"Red had now sighted us. Throughout the affair he showed a remarkably poor stomach for gun-fire, and this was his undoing. Moreover, he was tempted by the poorness of our cover on our right to attempt to outflank and enfilade us there. Accordingly, partly to get cover from our two central guns and partly to outflank us, he sent the whole of his left wing to the left of Firely Church, where, except for the gun, it became almost a negligible quantity. The gun came out between the church and the wood into a position from which it did a considerable amount of mischief to the infantry on our right, and nearly drove our rightmost gun in upon its supports. Meanwhile, Red's two guns on his right came forward to Hook's Farm, rather badly supported by his infantry.

"Once they got into position there I perceived that we should be done for, and accordingly I rushed every available man forward in a vigorous counter attack, and my own two guns came lumbering up to the farmhouse corners, and got into the wedge of shelter close behind the house before his could open fire. His fire met my advance, littering the gentle grass slope with dead, and then, hot behind the storm of shell, and even as my cavalry gathered to charge his guns, he charged mine. I was amazed beyond measure at that rush, knowing his sabres to be slightly outnumbered by mine. In another moment all the level space round the farmhouse was a whirling storm of slashing cavalry, and then we found ourselves still holding on, with half a dozen prisoners, and the farmyard a perfect shambles of horses and men. The melee was over. His charge had failed, and, after a brief breathing—space for my shot—torn infantry to come up, I led on the counter attack. It was brilliantly successful; a hard five minutes with bayonet and sabre, and his right gun was in our hands and his central one in jeopardy.

"And now Red was seized with that most fatal disease of generals, indecision. He would neither abandon his lost gun nor adequately attack it. He sent forward a feeble little infantry attack, that we cut up with the utmost ease, taking several prisoners, made a disastrous demonstration from the church, and then fell back altogether from the gentle hill on which Hook Farm is situated to a position beside and behind an exposed cottage on the level. I at once opened out into a long crescent, with a gun at either horn, whose crossfire completely destroyed his chances of retreat from this ill-chosen last stand, and there presently we disabled his second gun. I now turned my attention to his still largely unbroken right, from which a gun had maintained a galling fire on us throughout the fight. I might still have had some stiff work getting an attack home to the church, but Red had had enough of it, and now decided to relieve me of any further exertion by a precipitate retreat. My gun to the right of Hook's Farm killed three of his flying men, but my cavalry were too badly cut up for an effective pursuit, and he got away to the extreme left of his original positions with about 6 infantry-men, 4 cavalry, and 1 gun. He went none too soon. Had he stayed, it would have been only a question of time before we shot him to pieces and finished him altogether."

So far, and a little vaingloriously, the general. Let me now shrug my shoulders and shake him off, and go over this battle he describes a little more exactly with the help of the photographs. The battle is a small, compact game of the Fight-to-a-Finish type, and it was arranged as simply as possible in order to permit of a full and exact explanation.

FIG. 6a.—BATTLE OF HOOK'S FARM. Position of armies at end of Blue's third move. (*See page* 82.)

FIG. 7.—BATTLE OF HOOK'S FARM. Showing the frantic rush of Red's left wing across the open to join the main body. (*See page* 82.)

Figure 1 shows the country of the battlefield put out; on the right is the church, on the left (near the centre of the plate) is the farm. In the hollow between the two is a small outbuilding. Directly behind the farm in the line of vision is another outbuilding. This is more distinctly seen in other photographs. Behind, the chalk back line is clear. Red has won the toss, both for the choice of a side and, after making that choice, for first move, and his force is already put out upon the back line. For the sake of picturesqueness, the men are not put exactly on the line, but each will have his next move measured from that line. Red has broken his force into two, a fatal error, as we shall see, in view of the wide space of open ground between the farm and the church. He has 1 gun, 5 cavalry, and 13 infantry on his left, who are evidently to take up a strong position by the church and enfilade Blue's position; Red's right, of 2 guns, 20 cavalry, and 37 infantry aim at the seizure of the farm.

Figure 2 is a near view of Blue's side, with his force put down. He has grasped the strategic mistake of Red, and is going to fling every man at the farm. His right, of 5 cavalry and 16 infantry, will get up as soon as possible to the woods near the centre of the field (whence the fire of their gun will be able to cut off the two portions of Red's force from each other), and then, leaving the gun there with sufficient men to serve it, the rest of this party will push on to co-operate with the main force of their comrades in the inevitable scrimmage for the farm.

Figure 3 shows the fight after Red and Blue have both made their first move. It is taken from Red's side. Red has not as yet realised the danger of his position. His left gun struggles into position to the left of the church, his centre and right push for the farm. Blue's five cavalry on his left have already galloped forward into a favourable position to open fire at the next move—they are a little hidden in the picture by the church; the sixteen infantry follow hard, and his main force makes straight for the farm.

Figure 4 shows the affair developing rapidly. Red's cavalry on his right have taken his two guns well forward into a position to sweep either side of the farm, and his left gun is now well placed to pound Blue's infantry centre. His infantry continue to press forward, but Blue, for his second move, has already opened fire from the woods with his right gun, and killed three of Red's men. His infantry have now come up to serve this gun, and the cavalry who brought it into position at the first move have now left it to them in order to gallop over to join the force attacking the farm. Undismayed by Red's guns, Blue has brought his other two guns and his men as close to the farm as they can go. His leftmost gun stares Red's in the face, and prevents any effective fire, his middle gun faces Red's middle gun. Some of his cavalry are exposed to the right of the farm, but most are completely covered now by the farm from Red's fire. Red has now to move. The nature of his position is becoming apparent to him. His right gun is ineffective, his left and his centre guns cannot kill more than seven or eight men between them; and at the next move, unless he can silence them, Blue's guns will be mowing his exposed cavalry down from the security of the farm. He is in a fix. How is he to get out of it? His cavalry are slightly outnumbered, but he decides to do as much execution as he can with his own guns, charge the Blue guns before him, and then bring up his infantry to save the situation.

Figure 5a shows the result of Red's move. His two effective guns have between them bowled over two cavalry and six infantry in the gap between the farm and Blue's right gun; and then, following up the effect of his gunfire, his cavalry charges home over the Blue guns. One oversight he makes, to which Blue at once calls his attention at the end of his move. Red has reckoned on twenty cavalry for his charge, forgetting that by the rules he must put two men at the tail of his middle gun. His infantry are just not able to come up for this duty, and consequently two cavalry-men have to be set there. The game then pauses while the players work out the cavalry melee. Red has brought up eighteen men to this; in touch or within six inches of touch there are twenty-one Blue cavalry. Red's force is isolated, for only two of his men are within a move, and to support eighteen he would have to have nine. By the rules this gives fifteen men dead on either side and three Red prisoners to Blue. By the rules also it rests with Red to indicate the survivors within the limits of the melee as he chooses. He takes very good care there are not four men within six inches of either Blue gun, and both these are out of action therefore for Blue's next move. Of course Red would have done far better to have charged home with thirteen men only, leaving seven in support, but he was flurried by his comparatively unsuccessful shooting—he had wanted to hit more cavalry—and by the gun-trail mistake. Moreover, he had counted his antagonist wrongly, and thought he could arrange a melee of twenty against twenty.

Figure 5b shows the game at the same stage as 5a, immediately after the adjudication of the melee. The dead have been picked up, the three prisoners, by a slight deflection of the rules in the direction of the picturesque, turn their faces towards captivity, and the rest of the picture is exactly in the position of 5a.

It is now Blue's turn to move, and figure 6a shows the result of his move. He fires his rightmost gun (the nose of it is just visible to the right) and kills one infantry-man and one cavalry-man (at the tail of Red's central gun), brings up his surviving eight cavalry into convenient positions for the service of his temporarily silenced guns, and hurries his infantry forward to the farm, recklessly exposing them in the thin wood between the farm and his right gun. The attentive reader will be able to trace all this in figure 6a, and he will also note the three Red cavalry prisoners going to the rear under the escort of one Khaki infantry man.

Figure 6b shows exactly the same stage as figure 6a, that is to say, the end of Blue's third move. A cavalry-man lies dead at the tail of Red's middle gun, an infantry-man a little behind it. His rightmost gun is abandoned and partly masked, but not hidden, from the observer, by a tree to the side of the farmhouse.

And now, what is Red to do?

The reader will probably have his own ideas, as I have mine. What Red did do in the actual game was to lose his head, and then at the end of four minutes' deliberation he had to move, he blundered desperately. He opened fire on Blue's exposed centre and killed eight men. (Their bodies litter the ground in figure 7, which gives a complete bird's-eye view of the battle.) He then sent forward and isolated six or seven men in a wild attempt to recapture his lost gun, massed his other men behind the inadequate cover of his central gun, and sent the detachment of infantry that had hitherto lurked uselessly behind the church, in a frantic and hopeless rush across the open to join them. (The one surviving cavalry-man on his right wing will be seen taking refuge behind the cottage.) There can be little question of the entire unsoundness of all these movements. Red was at a disadvantage, he had failed to capture the farm, and his business now was manifestly to save his men as much as possible, make a defensive fight of it, inflict as much damage as possible with his leftmost gun on Blue's advance, get the remnants of his right across to the church—the cottage in the centre and their own gun would have given them a certain amount of cover—and build up a new position about that building as a pivot. With two guns right and left of the church he might conceivably have saved the rest of the fight.

That, however, is theory; let us return to fact. Figure 8 gives the disastrous consequences of Red's last move. Blue has moved, his guns have slaughtered ten of Red's wretched foot, and a rush of nine Blue cavalry and infantry mingles with Red's six surviving infantry about the disputed gun. These infantry by the definition are isolated; there are not three other Reds within a move of them. The view in this photograph also is an extensive one, and the reader will note, as a painful accessory, the sad spectacle of three Red prisoners receding to the right. The melee about Red's lost gun works out, of course, at three dead on each side, and three more Red prisoners.

Henceforth the battle moves swiftly to complete the disaster of Red. Shaken and demoralised, that unfortunate general is now only for retreat. His next move, of which I have no picture, is to retreat the infantry he has so wantonly exposed back to the shelter of the church, to withdraw the wreckage of his right into the cover of the cottage, and—one last gleam of enterprise—to throw forward his left gun into a position commanding Blue's right.

FIG. 8.—BATTLE OF HOOK'S FARM. The Red Army suffers heavy losses. (See page 83.)

FIG. 9.—BATTLE OF HOOK'S FARM. Complete victory of the Blue Army. (See page 83.)

Blue then pounds Red's right with his gun to the right of the farm and kills three men. He extends his other gun to the left of the farm, right out among the trees, so as to get an effective fire next time upon the tail of Red's gun. He also moves up sufficient men to take possession of Red's lost gun. On the right Blue's gun engages Red's and kills one man. All this the reader will see clearly in figure 9, and he will also note a second batch of Red prisoners—this time they are infantry, going rearward. Figure 9 is the last picture that is needed to tell the story of the battle. Red's position is altogether hopeless. He has four men left alive by his rightmost gun, and their only chance is to attempt to save that by retreating with it. If they fire it, one or other will certainly be killed at its tail in Blue's subsequent move, and then the gun will be neither movable nor fireable. Red's left gun, with four men only, is also in extreme peril, and will be immovable and helpless if it loses another man.

Very properly Red decided upon retreat. His second gun had to be abandoned after one move, but two of the men with it escaped over his back line. Five of the infantry behind the church escaped, and his third gun and its four cavalry got away on the extreme left-hand corner of Red's position. Blue remained on the field, completely victorious, with two captured guns and six prisoners.

There you have a scientific record of the worthy general's little affair.

• • •

V

EXTENSIONS AND AMPLIFICATIONS OF LITTLE WAR

Now that battle of Hook's Farm is, as I have explained, a simplification of the game, set out entirely to illustrate the method of playing; there is scarcely a battle that will not prove more elaborate (and eventful) than this little encounter. If a number of players and a sufficiently large room can be got, there is no reason why armies of many hundreds of soldiers should not fight over many square yards of model country. So long as each player has about a hundred men and three guns there is no need to lengthen the duration of a game on that account. But it is too laborious and confusing for a single player to handle more than that number of men.

Moreover, on a big floor with an extensive country it is possible to begin moving with moves double or treble the length here specified, and to come down to moves of the ordinary lengths when the troops are within fifteen or twelve or ten feet of each other. To players with the time and space available I would suggest using a quite large country, beginning with treble moves, and, with the exception of a select number of cavalry scouts, keeping the soldiers in their boxes with the lids on, and moving the boxes as units. (This boxing idea is a new one, and affords a very good substitute for the curtain; I have tried it twice for games in the open air where the curtain was not available.) Neither side would, of course, know what the other had in its boxes; they might be packed regiments or a mere skeleton force. Each side would advance on the other by double or treble moves behind a screen of cavalry scouts, until a scout was within ten feet of a box on the opposite side. Then the contents of that particular box would have to be disclosed and the men stood out. Troops without any enemy within twenty feet could be returned to their boxes for facility in moving. Playing on such a scale would admit also of the introduction of the problem of provisions and supplies. Little toy Army Service waggons can be bought, and it could be ruled that troops must have one such waggon for every fifty men within at least six moves. Moreover, ammunition carts may be got, and it may be ruled that one must be within two moves of a gun before the latter can be fired. All these are complications of the War Game, and so far I have not been able to get together sufficient experienced players to play on this larger, more elaborate scale. It is only after the smaller simpler war game here described has been played a number of times, and its little dodges mastered completely, that such more warlike devices become practicable.

But obviously with a team of players and an extensive country, one could have a general controlling the whole campaign, divisional commanders, batteries of guns, specialised brigades, and a quite military movement of the whole affair. I have (as several illustrations show) tried Little Wars in the open air. The toy soldiers stand quite well on closely mown grass, but the long-range gun-fire becomes a little uncertain if there is any breeze. It gives a greater freedom of movement and allows the players to lie down more comfortably when firing, to increase, and even double, the moves of the indoor game. One can mark out high roads and streams with an ordinary lawn-tennis marker, mountains and rocks of stones, and woods and forests of twigs are easily arranged. But if the game is to be left out all night and continued next day (a thing I have as yet had no time to try), the houses must be of some more solid material than paper. I would suggest painted blocks of wood. On a large lawn, a wide country-side may be easily represented. The players may begin with a game exactly like the ordinary Kriegspiel, with scouts and boxed soldiers, which will develop into such battles as are here described, as the troops come into contact. It would be easy to give the roads a real significance by permitting a move half as long again as in the open country for waggons or boxed troops along a road. There is a possibility of having a toy railway, with stations or rolling stock into which troops might be put, on such a giant war map. One would allow a move for entraining and another for detraining, requiring the troops to be massed alongside the train at the beginning and end of each journey, and the train might move at four or five times the cavalry rate. One would use open trucks and put in a specified number of men—say twelve infantry or five cavalry or half a gun per truck—and permit an engine to draw seven or eight trucks, or move at a reduced speed with more. One could also rule that four men—the same four men—remaining on a line during two moves, could tear up a rail, and eight men in three moves replace it.

I will confess I have never yet tried over these more elaborate developments of Little Wars, partly because of the limited time at my disposal, and partly because they all demand a number of players who are well acquainted with the same on each side if they are not to last interminably. The Battle of Hook's Farm (one player a side) took a whole afternoon, and most of my battles have lasted the better part of a day.

• • •

VI

ENDING WITH A SORT OF CHALLENGE

I Could go on now and tell of battles, copiously. In the memory of the one skirmish I have given I do but taste blood. I would like to go on, to a large, thick book. It would be an agreeable task. Since I am the chief inventor and practiser (so far) of Little Wars, there has fallen to me a disproportionate share of victories. But let me not boast. For the present, I have done all that I meant to do in this matter. It is for you, dear reader, now to get a floor, a friend, some soldiers and some guns, and show by a grovelling devotion your appreciation of this noble and beautiful gift of a limitless game that I have given you.

And if I might for a moment trumpet! How much better is this amiable miniature than the Real Thing! Here is a homeopathic remedy for the imaginative strategist. Here is the premeditation, the thrill, the strain of accumulating victory or disaster—and no smashed nor sanguinary bodies, no shattered fine buildings nor devastated country sides, no petty cruelties, none of that awful universal boredom and embitterment, that tiresome delay or stoppage or embarrassment of every gracious, bold, sweet, and charming thing, that we who are old enough to remember a real modern war know to be the reality of belligerence. This world is for ample living; we want security and freedom; all of us in every country, except a few dull-witted, energetic bores, want to see the manhood of the world at something better than apeing the little lead toys our children buy in boxes. We want fine things made for mankind—splendid cities, open ways, more knowledge and power, and more and more and more—and so I offer my game, for a particular as well as a general end; and let us put this prancing monarch and that silly scare-monger, and these excitable "patriots," and those adventurers, and all the practitioners of Welt Politik, into one vast Temple of War, with cork carpets everywhere, and plenty of little trees and little houses to knock down, and cities and fortresses, and unlimited soldiers—tons, cellars-full—and let them lead their own lives there away from us.

My game is just as good as their game, and saner by reason of its size. Here is War, done down to rational proportions, and yet out of the way of mankind, even as our fathers turned human sacrifices into the eating of little images and symbolic mouthfuls. For my own part, I am **prepared**. I have nearly five hundred men, more than a score of guns, and I twirl my moustache and hurl defiance eastward from my home in Essex across the narrow seas. Not only eastward. I would conclude this little discourse with one other disconcerting and exasperating sentence for the admirers and practitioners of Big War. I have never yet met in little battle any military gentleman, any captain, major, colonel, general, or eminent commander, who did not presently get into difficulties and confusions among even the elementary rules of the Battle. You have only to play at Little Wars three or four times to realise just what a blundering thing Great War must be.

Great War is at present, I am convinced, not only the most expensive game in the universe, but it is a game out of all proportion. Not only are the masses of men and material and suffering and inconvenience too monstrously big for reason, but—the available heads we have for it, are too small. That, I think, is the most pacific realisation conceivable, and Little War brings you to it as nothing else but Great War can do.

• • •

APPENDIX

LITTLE WARS AND KRIEGSPIEL

This little book has, I hope, been perfectly frank about its intentions. It is not a book upon Kriegspiel. It gives merely a game that may be played by two or four or six amateurish persons in an afternoon and evening with toy soldiers. But it has a very distinct relation to Kriegspiel; and since the main portion of it was written and published in a magazine, I have had quite a considerable correspondence with military people who have been interested by it, and who have shown a very friendly spirit towards it—in spite of the pacific outbreak in its concluding section. They tell me—what I already a little suspected—that Kriegspiel, as it is played by the British Army, is a very dull and unsatisfactory exercise, lacking in realism, in stir and the unexpected, obsessed by the umpire at every turn, and of very doubtful value in waking up the imagination, which should be its chief function. I am particularly indebted to Colonel Mark Sykes for advice and information in this matter. He has pointed out to me the possibility of developing Little Wars into a vivid and inspiring Kriegspiel, in which the element of the umpire would be reduced to a minimum; and it would be ungrateful to him, and a waste of an interesting opportunity, if I did not add this Appendix, pointing out how a Kriegspiel of real educational value for junior officers may be developed out of the amusing methods of Little War. If Great War is to be played at all, the better it is played the more humanely it will be done. I see no inconsistency in deploring the practice while perfecting the method. But I am a civilian, and Kriegspiel is not my proper business. I am deeply preoccupied with a novel I am writing, and so I think the best thing I can do is just to set down here all the ideas that have cropped up in my mind, in the footsteps, so to speak, of Colonel Sykes, and leave it to the military expert, if he cares to take the matter up, to reduce my scattered suggestions to a system.

Now, first, it is manifest that in Little Wars there is no equivalent for rifle-fire, and that the effect of the gun-fire has no resemblance to the effect of shell. That may be altered very simply. Let the rules as to gun-fire be as they are now, but let a different projectile be used—a projectile that will drop down and stay where it falls. I find that one can buy in ironmongers' shops small brass screws of various sizes and weights, but all capable of being put in the muzzle of the 4'7 guns without slipping down the barrel. If, with such a screw in the muzzle, the gun is loaded and fired, the wooden bolt remains in the gun and the screw flies and drops and stays near where it falls—its range being determined by the size and weight of screw selected by the gunner. Let us assume this is a shell, and it is quite easy to make a rule that will give the effect of its explosion. Half, or, in the case of an odd number, one more than half, of the men within three inches of this shell are dead, and if there is a gun completely within the circle of three inches radius from the shell, it is destroyed. If it is not completely within the circle, it is disabled for two moves. A supply waggon is completely destroyed if it falls wholly or partially within the radius. But if there is a wall, house, or entrenchment between any men and the shell, they are uninjured—they do not count in the reckoning of the effect of the shell.

I think one can get a practical imitation of the effect of rifle-fire by deciding that for every five infantry-men who are roughly in a line, and who do not move in any particular move, there may be one (ordinary) shot taken with a 4'7 gun. It may be fired from any convenient position behind the row of five men, so long as the shot passes roughly over the head of the middle man of the five.

Of course, while in Little Wars there are only three or four players, in any proper Kriegspiel the game will go on over a larger area—in a drill-hall or some such place—and each arm and service will be entrusted to a particular player. This permits all sorts of complicated imitations of reality that are impossible to our parlour and playroom Little Wars. We can consider transport, supply, ammunition, and the moral effect of cavalry impact, and of uphill and downhill movements. We can also bring in the spade and entrenchment, and give scope to the Royal Engineers. But before I write anything of Colonel Sykes' suggestions about these, let me say a word or two about Kriegspiel "country."

The country for Kriegspiel should be made up, I think, of heavy blocks or boxes of wood about 3 x 3 x 1/2 feet, and curved pieces (with a rounded outline and a chord of three feet, or shaped like right-angled triangles with an incurved hypotenuse and two straight sides of 3 feet) can easily be contrived to round off corners and salient angles. These blocks can be bored to take trees, etc., exactly as the boards in Little Wars are bored, and with them a very passable model of any particular country can be built up from a contoured Ordnance map. Houses may be made very cheaply by shaping a long piece of wood into a house-like section and sawing it up. There will always be someone who will touch up and paint and stick windows on to and generally adorn and individualise such houses, which are, of course, the stabler the heavier the wood used. The rest of the country as in Little Wars.

Upon such a country a Kriegspiel could be played with rules upon the lines of the following sketch rules, which are the result of a discussion between Colonel Sykes and myself, and in which most of the new ideas are to be ascribed to Colonel Sykes. We proffer them, not as a finished set of rules, but as material for anyone who chooses to work over them, in the elaboration of what we believe will be a far more exciting and edifying Kriegspiel than any that exists at the present time. The game may be played by any number of players, according to the forces engaged and the size of the country available. Each side will be under the supreme command of a General, who will be represented by a cavalry soldier. The player who is General must stand at or behind his representative image and within six feet of it. His signalling will be supposed to be perfect, and he will communicate with his subordinates by shout, whisper, or note, as he thinks fit. I suggest he should be considered invulnerable, but Colonel Sykes has proposed arrangements for his disablement. He would have it that if the General falls within the zone of destruction of a shell he must go out of the room for three moves (injured); and that if he is hit by rifle-fire or captured he shall quit the game, and be succeeded by his next subordinate.

Now as to the Moves.

It is suggested that:

Infantry shall move one foot.

Cavalry shall move three feet.

The above moves are increased by one half for troops in twos or fours on a road.

Royal Engineers shall move two feet.

Royal Artillery shall move two feet.

Transport and Supply shall move one foot on roads, half foot across country.

The General shall move six feet (per motor), three feet across country.

Boats shall move one foot.

In moving uphill, one contour counts as one foot; downhill, two contours count as one foot. Where there are four contours to one foot vertical the hill is impassable for wheels unless there is a road.

Infantry.

To pass a fordable river = one move.

To change from fours to two ranks = half a move.

To change from two ranks to extension = half a move.

To embark into boats = two moves for every twenty men embarked at any point.

To disembark = one move for every twenty men.

Cavalry.

To pass a fordable river = one move.

To change formation = half a move.

To mount = one move.

To dismount = one move.

Artillery.

To unlimber guns = half a move.

To limber up guns = half a move.

Rivers are impassable to guns.

NEITHER INFANTRY, CAVALRY, NOR ARTILLERY CAN FIRE AND MOVE IN ONE MOVE.

Royal Engineers.

No repairs can be commenced, no destructions can be begun, during a move in which R.E. have changed position.

Rivers impassable.

Transport and Supply.

No supplies or stores can be delivered during a move if T. and S. have moved.

Rivers impassable.

Next as to Supply in the Field:

All troops must be kept supplied with food, ammunition, and forage. The players must give up, every six moves, one packet of food per thirty men; one packet of forage per six horses; one packet of ammunition per thirty infantry which fire for six consecutive moves.

These supplies, at the time when they are given up, must be within six feet of the infantry they belong to and eighteen feet of the cavalry.

Isolated bodies of less than thirty infantry require no supplies—a body is isolated if it is more than twelve feet off another body. In calculating supplies for infantry the fractions either count as thirty if fifteen or over, or as nothing if less than fifteen. Thus forty-six infantry require two packets of food or ammunition; forty-four infantry require one packet of food.

N.B.—Supplies are not effective if enemy is between supplies and troops they belong to.

Men surrounded and besieged must be victualled at the following rate:—

One packet food for every thirty men for every six moves.

One packet forage every six horses for every six moves.

In the event of supplies failing, horses may take the place of food, but not of course of forage; one horse to equal one packet.

In the event of supplies failing, the following consequences ensue:—

Infantry without ammunition cannot fire (guns are supposed to have unlimited ammunition with them).

Infantry, cavalry, R.A., and R.E. cannot move without supply—if supplies are not provided within six consecutive moves, they are out of action.

A force surrounded must surrender four moves after eating its last horse.

Now as to Destructions:

To destroy a railway bridge R.E. take two moves; to repair, R.E. take ten moves.

To destroy a railway culvert R.E. take one move; to repair R.E. take five moves. To destroy a river road bridge R.E. take one move; to repair, R.E. take five moves.

A supply depot can be destroyed by one man in two moves, no matter how large (by fire).

Four men can destroy the contents of six waggons in one move.

A contact mine can be placed on a road or in any place by two men in six moves; it will be exploded by the first pieces passing over it, and will destroy everything within six inches radius.*

Next as to Constructions:

Entrenchments can be made by infantry in four moves.* They are to be strips of wood two inches high tacked to the country, or wooden bricks two inches high. Two men may make an inch of entrenchment.

Epaulements for guns may be constructed at the rate of six men to one epaulement in four moves.*

[* Notice to be given to umpire of commencement of any work or the placing of a mine. In event of no umpire being available, a folded note must be put on the mantelpiece when entrenchment is commenced, and opponent asked to open it when the trench is completed or the mine exploded.]

Rules as to Cavalry Charging:

No body of less than eight cavalry may charge, and they must charge in proper formation.

If cavalry charges infantry in extended order—

If the charge starts at a distance of more than two feet, the cavalry loses one man for every five infantry-men charged, and the infantry loses one man for each sabre charging.

At less than two feet and more than one foot, the cavalry loses one man for every ten charged, and the infantry two men for each sabre charging.

At less than one foot, the cavalry loses one man for every fifteen charged, and the infantry three men for each sabre charging.

If cavalry charges infantry in close order, the result is reversed.

Thus at more than two feet one infantry-man kills three cavalry-men, and fifteen cavalry-men one infantry-man.

At more than one foot one infantry-man kills two cavalry, and ten cavalry one infantry.

At less than one foot one infantry-man kills one cavalry, and five cavalry one infantry.

However, infantry that have been charged in close order are immobile for the subsequent move.

Infantry charged in extended order must on the next move retire one foot; they can be charged again.

If cavalry charges cavalry:—

If cavalry is within charging distance of the enemy's cavalry at the end of the enemy's move, it must do one of three things—dismount, charge, or retire. If it remains stationary and mounted and the enemy charges, one charging sabre will kill five stationary sabres and put fifteen others three feet to the rear.

Dismounted cavalry charged is equivalent to infantry in extended order.

If cavalry charges cavalry and the numbers are equal and the ground level, the result must be decided by the toss of a coin; the loser losing three-quarters of his men and obliged to retire, the winner losing one-quarter of his men.

If the numbers are unequal, the melee rules for Little Wars obtain if the ground is level.

If the ground slopes, the cavalry charging downhill will be multiplied according to the number of contours crossed. If it is one contour, it must be multiplied by two; two contours, multiplied by three; three contours, multiplied by four.

If cavalry retires before cavalry instead of accepting a charge, it must continue to retire so long as it is pursued—the pursuers can only be arrested by fresh cavalry or by infantry or artillery fire.

If driven off the field or into an unfordable river, the retreating body is destroyed.

If infantry find hostile cavalry within charging distance at the end of the enemy's move, and this infantry retires and yet is still within charging distance, it will receive double losses if in extended order if charged; and if in two ranks or in fours, will lose at three feet two men for each charging sabre; at two feet, three men for each charging sabre.

The cavalry in these circumstances will lose nothing. The infantry will have to continue to retire until their tormentors have exterminated them or been driven off by someone else.

If cavalry charges artillery and is not dealt with by other forces, one gun is captured with a loss to the cavalry of four men per gun for a charge at three feet, three men at two feet, and one man at one foot.

If artillery retires before cavalry when cavalry is within charging distance, it must continue to retire so long as the cavalry pursues.

The introduction of toy railway trains, moving, let us say, eight feet per move, upon toy rails, needs rules as to entraining and detraining and so forth, that will be quite easily worked out upon the model of boat embarkation here given. An engine or truck within the circle of destruction of a shell will be of course destroyed.

The toy soldiers used in this Kriegspiel should not be the large soldiers used in Little Wars. The British manufacturers who turn out these also make a smaller, cheaper type of man—the infantry about an inch high—which is better adapted to Kriegspiel purposes.

We hope, if these suggestions "catch on," to induce them to manufacture a type of soldier more exactly suited to the needs of the game, including tray carriers for troops in formation and (what is at present not attainable) dismountable cavalry that will stand.

We place this rough sketch of a Kriegspiel entirely at the disposal of any military men whose needs and opportunities enable them to work it out and make it into an exacter and more realistic game. In doing so, we think they will find it advisable to do their utmost to make the game work itself, and to keep the need for umpire's decisions at a minimum. Whenever possible, death should be by actual gun- and rifle-fire and not by computation. Things should happen, and not be decided. We would also like to insist upon the absolute need of an official upon either side, simply to watch and measure the moves taken, and to collect and check the amounts of supply and ammunition given up. This is a game like real war, played against time, and played under circumstances of considerable excitement, and it is remarkable how elastic the measurements of quite honest and honourable men can become.

We believe that the nearer that Kriegspiel approaches to an actual small model of war, not only in its appearance but in its emotional and intellectual tests, the better it will serve its purpose of trial and education.

The End.

BOOKS PUBLISHED BY
PHAROS BOOKS